Peter the Pixie goes to School

Rhymes by Maureen Spurgeon
Illustrations by Hildrun Covi

Published by
W.F. Graham (Northampton) Ltd

Peter the Pixie feels such sorrow
As Daddy says: "School starts tomorrow!
There you must work, as well as play,
And do your lessons, every day!
Before too long, you'll find you need
To add up sums and write and read!"

"There's your school – now, can you see?
In the shade of that green tree!
Teacher will be waiting there –
You need not have a single care!
You'll make new friends who'll go there, too.
And learning will be good for you!

covi

Next day, Peter peeped inside.
"What Daddy said was true!" he cried.
"There's the hedgehog family!
And four tits chatter, full of glee!
Those baby mice will soon feel well . . .
And that sounds like Hare's bicycle bell!"

covi

He sits near the door – clever thinking!
Then he'll be away, quick as blinking!
Feet on desk, he whistles and hums –
But then, quite soon, the teacher comes.
"Welcome to my school!" he said.
"But, Peter – sing a song, instead!"

covi

"I can sing, too!" grumbles Bear.
"I must join in, or it's not fair!"
Teacher says: "Your voice is gruff!
You grunt and growl, that's not enough!
So just sit down, and listen to me.
There are more things to learn, you'll see!"

1+2=3
3-2=
COVI

Just as he spoke, three tiny bees
Buzzed into class, calm as you please!
Peter the Pixie hears Teacher shout:
“You’re all much too small! You must go out!
Come to my school once you start to grow!”
And how they all laugh at bees buzzing so!

COVI

Now, lessons start, with sums to be done.
For Peter the Pixie, that isn't much fun.
When Teacher tells him to add four and four,
He thinks it's seven! He must try once more!
"Don't worry!" says Teacher. "Check up your sums
By counting across your fingers and thumbs!"

3+ 3 = 6
4+4=
4+4=7
COVI

Some reading, and then they all go outside.
Peter the Pixie takes Hare's snack to hide!
Hare is quite cross. "I'll give you a smack,
Peter the Pixie! So, just hand it back!"
Their laughter at play-time sounds through the wood –
Being at school is really quite good!

covi

Home-time, now – so out they all run.
The first day at school has been lots of fun.
"Goodbye!" calls Teacher, with smiles and a wave.
"Go straight home! And mind you behave!
I'll see you tomorrow, we'll learn something new!
And I'll be so happy to see all of you!"

COVI

COVI